The Great Adventures of

Regina and Richey

— The Gift —

Sandra L. Brenk

AuthorHouse™
1663 Liberty Drive
Bloomington, IN 47403
www.authorhouse.com
Phone: 833-262-8899

Because of the dynamic nature of the Internet, any web addresses or links contained in this book may have changed
since publication and may no longer be valid. The views expressed in this work are solely those of the author and do not
necessarily reflect the views of the publisher, and the publisher hereby disclaims any responsibility for them.

This book is printed on acid-free paper.

ISBN: 978-1-4520-0787-8 (sc)

Library of Congress Control Number: 2015901975

Print information available on the last page.

Published by AuthorHouse 06/06/2022

authorHOUSE®

The Great Adventures of Regina and Richey

"Hey there, Regina!" shouted Richey. Everyone else in school called Richey "Riches." I suppose that name sort of fit because his family was wealthy and had an upscale lifestyle. My nickname was "Rags." It was first given to me about five years ago when I started second grade. The kids teased me and said that it looked like my mom had dressed me up in an outfit she had made out of old rags.

As you can tell, the name stuck. My mom couldn't afford to buy me or my little brother, Matt, a lot of fancy things. But we rarely ever went without socks or undergarments. She was a good mom, so we wore whatever she wanted us to, and we did it with little complaint. We knew she was doing her best and it would only hurt her feelings if we complained. I wore the dresses my mom made and took the ridicule that came with it. People made fun of me because I looked different and I didn't dress like the popular girls in my class.

When our classmates saw Richey and me hanging out together, they just couldn't resist the temptation to name us "Rags to Riches." How silly, I thought, but I liked it in an odd sort of way. Richey and I were the best of friends. We were like salt and pepper; neither one of us was complete without the other.

Richey didn't seem to mind that our family didn't have as much money as his family had. Actually, I think that's what made our friendship so interesting.

If I were to give a description of me, I would have to say that my hair looks as though I stuck my finger in an electric socket. It's black, wiry, and definitely untamable. My legs look like two pale, knobby walking sticks. The rest of my body reflects the same ill color of my legs.

Richey, on the other hand, has globs of curly blond hair, tan skin, and dimples you want to squeeze. He was very popular in school, and most of the girls thought he was dreamy.

On this particular day, all the students in our school gathered in the gymnasium to participate in the yearly Christmas party. The students and teachers stood around laughing and chatting, drinking Kool-Aid and eating cookies, anticipating the surprises that were waiting in the various boxes and bags sitting under the tree. As the clock struck noon, we all hurried to our chairs. In the center of the gym stood the six-foot tall keeper of our packages—the Christmas tree, decorated with plenty of ornaments and blinking lights. The roar of excitement began; it was time to open presents.

Richey had told me about all the great gifts that he had picked out for everyone, everyone's gift except mine. He said I would have to open mine to see what it was.

While other people were exchanging gifts, Richey handed me my present and begged me to open it right away. I tore open my decorative package, and inside the little box sat a tiny, pink teddy bear. As I stared at the stuffed figure, I noticed the shiny object that was wrapped around the foot of the bear. It was a gold ring with a ruby sitting in the corner of a heart. It was beautiful, and it caused tears to well up in my eyes.

"But, Richey, I didn't … I mean …" I was at a loss for words and felt hot tears rolling down my face. I was filled with mixed emotions and became suddenly aware that my gift for Richey would fail in comparison. Richey stood there beaming at me, knowing that I was truly surprised by his gift. But then his cheerful smile faded as he watched my stare fall to the floor.

"Rags," he said hesitantly. "Don't you like it?" I tried to speak but wasn't able to push the words past my throat. I tried to look up at him, but I couldn't bear to see his eyes. I turned away and ran out of the gym, feeling as though I had somehow let him down. The gift I had for him wouldn't cause such excitement or emotion; it wasn't nearly as glamorous or as beautiful. I couldn't even stay to watch him open his present.

I ran toward the bathroom as fast as I could, embracing the bear and clutching the ring. I stopped short of the entrance and turned around. Did I care for Richey as much as he cared for me? How could I have chosen such a silly gift when he picked out such an extraordinary one for me? I knew that I wouldn't be able to return to the gym, so without another thought, I went to the nurse's office. I told Mrs. Helen, the nurse, that I wasn't feeling well, and I asked if I could stay in the office until it was time to go home. She smiled at me and nodded her head, so I slowly walked into the backroom and lay down. I couldn't stop thinking about Richey as I stared at my ring. I slowly put the ring on my finger, and then the tears began to fall again.

After the last bell rang, I left Mrs. Helen's office and slowly made my way down the hall. Most of the kids were long gone by now; only a few bookworms and teachers were left roaming the endless territory of knowledge.

I knew in my heart that any gift from Richey would have been special, but it felt like he went way overboard. I could never match such an extravagant gesture. I left school, and as I walked home, I thought more about the gift I had made Richey. My gift to him was somewhat unexciting compared to the gift that he had given me. My treasure for my friend was simple. I made him a plaque, although it was no ordinary plaque. I took a piece of board the size of an eight-by-ten picture frame. I only had to think for a moment about what I wanted it to say; that part was easy. Preparing the rough piece of wood was a little more of a challenge. Next, I picked out my favorite picture of me and Richey.

I then had to decide exactly where I would place the photo I chose. The inscription that I would puncture into the wood would have to be perfect because any errors were not fixable once done. I lightly sanded the board and wrote out the inscription in pencil. Once I was satisfied with the look of the letters and was almost certain that it would be easy to read, I began the task of tapping the nail into the wood along the letters I had written.

That part took a lot of patience and concentration. I had to be careful not to put the holes too close together, and I had to make sure I never went out of the line; otherwise the letters wouldn't look right. Two hours later, the tapping job was complete. I went over the board again several times with the sandpaper, smoothing out small pieces of splinters that had formed from the nail holes in the wood.

The board was now ready to be stained. In order to do that, I would have to go across the street to Mr. Thompson's house and borrow some of his supplies. I had already asked about using his things before I had even begun this project. I wanted to make sure I would be able to accomplish my goal even before I began.

I went to Mr. Thompson's house later that evening to show him my progress. He was pleased with my work and eager to help in my time of need. I had watched Mr. Thompson on several occasions staining small tables, boxes, and many other things that he had made. This was his hobby, and he enjoyed it. He supplied me with a paintbrush, the staining liquid, a roll of paper towels, and a pair of rubber gloves to help keep my hands clean.

I stroked the brush back and forth, dipping it into the can of liquid several times. I waited until the liquid stopped soaking into the wood before I wiped away the excess. Stain is a liquid that soaks into wood to help darken the color of it. This brings out the natural patterns and aging marks that are in the wood.

I left my project at Mr. Thompson's house for the night so it could dry, and I told him that I would return the next day to retrieve it. I then cleaned up my workstation and thanked him for his time and help. I went home excited about the results, and I couldn't wait to see how it was going to look once I placed the picture on it.

The picture was of me and Richey out on the lake. We had been sitting on the edge of the bank, laughing and not concentrating much on our fishing poles, when a fish yanked Richey's pole right out of his hands. He made such a funny face as he stared into the water. The shock only lasted a brief second, and then the urge to laugh exploded, and out came a roar of giggles. His mom had been standing nearby, and hearing the outburst, she snapped a few pictures as her son laughed with pure enjoyment. We had the best time that day, and I knew that picture would bring back good memories, so I asked Richey's mom for a copy of the picture.

The day after I stained the wood, I rushed over to Mr. Thompson's house to pick up my board, and then I hurried home to complete my project. I mounted the picture onto the wood in the upper left-hand corner. And beneath the photo, I placed a small slip of paper. It read: *Love, Rags.*

Mr. Thompson had given me a thin piece of plastic to cover the face of the board and protect the picture, so I inserted two small screws to hold the cover in place, and then the gift was complete. I was proud of my idea and beamed as I showed my mother what I had done. She smiled and said that Richey would love it. My heart warmed with that thought, and I carefully wrapped the gift in a box.

I remember feeling antsy and barely being able to wait for Christmas to arrive. I took my gift to school with me for the class Christmas party, and I was full of pride as I anticipated Richey's reaction. But the anticipation died shortly after I unwrapped his gift for me. Why had he done that? The gift I had been so proud to give him now seemed lame.

I finally made it to my room, and as soon as my head hit the pillows on my bed, my thoughts were interrupted by a familiar voice speaking to me. "Honey, are you okay?" my mother asked. "I got a call from the nurse today. She said that you weren't feeling well."

"I'm all right," I said as I sat up on my bed. "It's nothing for you to be worried about. I just felt a little under the weather, so I went to her office to lie down." I tried to wiggle my way out of the conversation without giving myself away.

"So, did Richey like his gift?" she asked.

"I didn't get a chance to watch him open it," I mumbled.

"But, honey, you worked so hard on that. Were you feeling so awful that you couldn't be there to watch him open his present?" A puzzled look appeared on her face. "What did he get you? Did you get a chance to open it?" More questions poured out of the now curious woman.

With my head lowered, attempting to avoid her stare, I said, "Yes, ma'am, I did."

"Well, do I get to see it or are you going to leave me in suspense?" she asked.

"Here, Mom, here's my gift." I lifted my hand up and showed her my new ring.

"How precious, Regina. He obviously thinks a lot about you to give you such a special gift," she said.

"I know—" My words were cut short as my brother came running into my room.

"Gina, Richey's here and he wants to know if you're all right." Before I could reply, my mother told Matt to let Richey in and to tell him where we were. Without delay, Matt was off to deliver the message.

"Mom!" I said, "I don't want to see him right now!"

"Regina, what's going on?" Her eyes squinted as she placed her hands on her hips.

"I just don't want to talk to him right now!" Just then, I glanced over to my bedroom door that was left open, and there stood a familiar figure with a hurt look on his face. I hadn't meant for him to hear my pleading with my mother. I just wanted some time to gather my thoughts.

"Regina, I don't know what's going on, but you're acting like a three-year-old instead of a ten-year-old. You need to start talking, and I mean right now. And you can start by apologizing to this young man." She was a loving mother, but she had no tolerance for nonsense.

"It's my gift, Mom! I gave him a stupid gift!" I explained with frustration.

"What?" she said. "But, Regina, you worked so hard on that plaque. You put a lot of thought and effort into it, and I can't imagine anyone not loving it, especially Richey."

Our stares turned to Richey; we were both waiting for confirmation that my mother was right.

"Rags, I loved my gift. I showed it to everyone in the class. Even the stuck-up girls looked at it with jealousy. I feel very lucky to have a friend who would make something so wonderful for me."

I suddenly felt very silly. A smile sneaked out from the corner of my mouth. "Did you really like it?" I questioned.

"I showed it to my mom, and it made her eyes water. She said that I was really lucky to have a friend like you."

"I'm sorry, Richey. I just thought that since you gave me such an expensive gift, my present would be disappointing to you. I felt like I had let you down."

"No, Rags. It's the best gift ever. And that's why we're best friends, because we care so much about each other. You're the best, Rags! And anyone would be proud to be friends with you. I know I am." He smiled.

"See, honey," my mom said. "Sometimes we just need to talk things out before jumping to conclusions. A silly misunderstanding can cause a lot of damage when we don't communicate."

"Rags and Riches sitting in a tree, k-i-s-s-i-n-g," Matt sang as he came running through the bedroom door.

"Mom, will you *please* take him with you!" I begged.

My mother gave me a kiss on the cheek and patted Richey on the shoulder. "I love you both," she said, and off she went playfully dragging Matt behind her.

We hugged each other, and then Richey began telling me about all the gifts that our classmates had given each other—and how none of them were as special as the one I had given him.

About the Author

I am someone who has always aspired to write a children's book. I love children and believe they should be given every opportunity to learn and be taught the skills needed to succeed in this world. I believe loving and protecting children is why we are here in the first place. My hope is that a child reads my book and comes away from it enlightened and better equipped in dealing with everyday trials. Life is a hard lesson and if I can teach a thing or two while entertaining a child through reading, than I feel I have contributed something to our future generations. And that's what life is all about, giving back and making life better for those that walk behind us.

Printed in the United States
by Baker & Taylor Publisher Services